INTRODUCTION

My name is Dorothy Ann — D.A. for short. I am one of the kids in Ms. Frizzle's class.

Maybe you have heard of Ms. Frizzle. (Sometimes we just call her the Friz.) She is a terrific teacher — but strange. One of her favorite subjects is science, and she knows everything about it.

She takes us on lots of field trips in the Magic School Bus. Believe me, it's not called *magic* for nothing! We never know what's going to happen when we get on that bus.

Ms. Frizzle likes to surprise us, but we

can usually tell when she is planning a spe-cial lesson — we just look at what she's wearing.

One day she came into class looking like she was going on a safari or something. She had on sturdy boots, a khaki jacket and pants with little kangaroos and other animals printed all over them, and a big hat. I knew we were in for a great time!

CHAPTER 1

"I love the end of January. We won't have any big holidays for a while," Arnold said, looking at our big wall calendar. He was right. We were in the last week of January and the calendar was completely blank.

"Why is that good?" I asked. "We always have really great trips around the holidays."

"Exactly!" said Arnold. "I'm looking forward to some nice, normal days in the classroom."

Just then, Ms. Frizzle came hopping in the door. "Good morning, class!" she sang out. "Happy Australia Day!"

"Oh, no!" Arnold groaned when he saw

her special outfit. "I shouldn't have said anything."

"What are you smiling about, D.A.?" Phoebe asked.

I was glad she had asked. I held up a copy of an Australia field guide. "I've just been reading about all the interesting wildlife in Australia," I told the class. I was in charge of our class project on wildlife for our school's annual science fair. I love science. I keep my science notebooks and the medal I won at last year's science fair with me all the time.

"Australia has some of the most unusual wildlife anywhere!" I told the class.

"That's righto, mate," Ms. Frizzle said. "Can you tell the class why that is?"

Aussie Dictionary

RIGHTO/RIGHTIO: All right, okay

"Because Australia is completely separated from any other land, so species there developed differently than in the rest of the world," I said proudly.

"That means Australia is a very different place," said the Friz.

Australia, a Country Apart
                                          by D.A.

Australia has many kinds of animals that don't live on other continents. Once there was a bridge of land that connected Australia with Asia. It disappeared about 30 million years ago. From then on, Australia's animal life didn't mix with the rest of the world. Australia is the only country that is its own continent.

"Who has heard of a dingo, wallaby, or wombat?" Ms. Frizzle asked.

I was the only one who raised my hand. "I've heard of a wallaby," I said. "It's a small kangaroo."

"How about a numbat, echidna, or kook-aburra?"

"I've heard of a kookaburra!" Phoebe said excitedly. "But I don't know what it is."

"I've heard of a kookaburra, too," said Arnold. "What is it?"

I had to admit I didn't know. I opened the Australia field guide and turned the pages. But I couldn't find a listing for "kook-aburra!"

"I think I've heard of it, too," said Ralphie while I was hunting through the field guide. "Isn't there a song about the kook-aburra?"

"That's right, Ralphie," said the Friz. "Let's sing the kookaburra song to start our Australia Day celebration!"

"What is Australia Day, anyway?" asked Tim.

Phoebe looked at me and I shrugged my shoulders.

"Australia Day marks the arrival of the first settlers in Australia. Australians always celebrate Australia Day on January twenty-sixth. And that's today. All right, class, let's sing the kookaburra song!" said the Friz.

Kookaburra sits in the old gum tree.
Merry, merry king of the bush is he,
Laugh, kookaburra, laugh, kookaburra,
Gay your life must be.

We practiced the song together until we all knew it, and then we split up into groups and sang in rounds. Phoebe loves to sing, and she looked happy. Arnold looked pretty gloomy. I know he doesn't like to sing — and the Friz's safari outfit had him worried.

"What is a kookaburra anyway, Ms. Frizzle?" Tim asked. "It sounds like some kind of a crazy bear!"

Ms. Frizzle took a tape recorder out of her safari bag. "Here is a tape of a kookaburra laughing," said the Friz. She pushed a button on the recorder and suddenly the room was filled with an eerie, crazy laughing sound.

"It must be an Australian monster!" said Arnold.

"Or a giant laughing lizard!" said Ralphie. Liz looked a little insulted.

"It sounds like a ghost," said Keesha.

"Maybe it's just a funny person who likes to eat berries," said Phoebe, looking at me.

"Are you sure it's real, Ms. Frizzle?" I asked. "I can't find an entry for kookaburra in my Australia field guide."

"May I see your book for a moment, Dorothy Ann?" Ms. Frizzle asked. She peered down at the book with me. "I think you're missing a page," she said. I looked closer. She

was right — a page had fallen out of the book! I shrugged my shoulders again. That made two mysteries: What was a kookaburra, and where had the missing page gone? Wanda thought of another one.

"What is a gum tree?" asked Wanda. "Is it sticky?"

"Just one of the many unusual and wonderful things in the land down under!" Ms. Frizzle said.

"Down under?" asked Arnold. "As in underground?"

The Friz lifted up the class globe, spun it so that the United States disappeared over the top, and pointed to a big island on the bottom of the globe. "That is Australia, and people who don't live there call it 'down under.' It is in the southern hemisphere, the half of Earth that's south of the equator."

Arnold looked happy. "Oh. That's really far away. Much too far for a field trip," he said under his breath.

8

"Oh, it is very far!" said the Friz. "But it's not too far to go to learn something new! Let's track down the kookaburra and find out what it is. Class, to the bus!"

Ms. Frizzle hopped out of the room, humming the kookaburra song. I threw my Australia field guide and my *Aussie Dictionary* into my bag and followed. You never know what you'll need on one of the Friz's trips. Maybe we'd need the dictionary to talk to the kookaburra. I couldn't wait to learn more about the land down under!

Aussie Dictionary

AUSSIE: Australia; Australian

CHAPTER 2

As soon as we got into the Magic School Bus and fastened our seat belts, we heard a roaring sound. The bus had become the Magic School Jet. "We never took jet trips at my old school," Phoebe yelled over the sound of the engines.

"As my uncle Mel Burn always said, 'If you've got somewhere to get, better take a jet!'" the Friz said with a laugh. We practiced our kookaburra song while the jet sped through the sky. Ms. Frizzle handed out snacks and read us an adventure story about some kids in Australia. Later, Liz passed out blankets and pillows and we all took naps.

When we woke up, we could see lots of hazy blue ocean below us. "Look out your windows," Ms. Frizzle called. "Who can spot Australia?"

I saw a gray shape in the distance. "There it is, there it is!" I yelled. I felt the plane tipping down.

"Back to your seats for landing," called the Friz.

I watched carefully out the window as we landed. We were passing mainland Australia and going to a smaller island south of Australia.

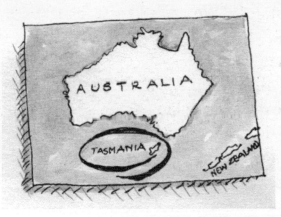

As the Magic School Jet landed, we saw that a very tall woman with very long black hair was there to greet us. "Welcome to Tasmania," she said as she climbed aboard. She grinned at us.

"Tiki!" said the Friz. "Thank you for meeting us here! Class, this is my good friend Tiki Hulme, who will be our Australian tour guide." Any friend of the Friz's was sure to be neat.

"Tiki lives here in Tasmania, so that's

why we came here first. I think she'll be able to help us find a kookaburra. She has a very special way with animals." We all looked at one another. When the Friz says "very special," she usually means it! We looked at Tiki with even more interest.

"Does the kookaburra live in Tasmania?" asked Wanda.

"The kookaburra lives mostly on Mainland Oz, although sometimes it gets as far south as here. But there are a lot of other interesting animals here. Let me introduce you to some of my friends."

Aussie Dictionary

OZ: Australia

Ms. Frizzle pushed a button, and the Magic School Jet became the Magic School Jeep. As soon as Tiki sat down, we took off down a grassy trail. "Please reach under your seats for your safari sighting packs," said the Friz. "We've got some sights to see!"

I took out my pack. Inside were a pair of field binoculars, a disposable camera, a bottle of water, and some raisins, peanuts, crackers, and cheese. Yum. Field rations.

We hadn't gone very far when Tiki vaulted over the side of the jeep. Ms. Frizzle brought the jeep to a screaming halt. I looked to see if Tiki was all right, but she was already running down a path. We piled out and followed after her. When we found her, she was standing in front of a flat rock. She pointed to a brownish cube on top of the rock. "Aha!" she said. "Anyone know what this is?"

"A brown block?" Carlos said doubtfully.

Tiki was so excited she didn't even hear Carlos. "This is wombat dung." We all looked blank. "This is how wombats mark their territory. They make their dung square so it won't roll off a flat surface. There should be a wombat not too far from here." She walked briskly off into the grassland. We followed quietly. Soon she pointed to some footprints in a sandy area. "He's close," she whispered. A second later she reached down and scooped up a big, furry creature that looked sort of like an oversized bear cub. The creature had been napping, and was now blinking sleepily at us. "This is a wombat," she said. "They're not usually out during the day. This fella should be asleep in his burrow." Several cameras clicked.

"He's kind of cute," Phoebe said. Arnold was peering at the wombat from behind her. Liz crawled out of Ms. Frizzle's bag for a closer look. I snapped a picture.

"He's a pretty gentle guy. Wombats only eat grasses and plants. They can hardly see, but they have excellent senses of smell and hearing. Notice how bristly his backside is. This shields him from predators when he's sleeping in his burrow. If a predator attempts to get into the burrow and tries to climb over him, Mr Wombat simply crushes him against the roof of his burrow. And look at these teeth." She opened the wombat's mouth. "They never stop growing, so they never get ground down." Tiki put the blinking wombat down. "Let's let him get back to sleep. OK, back to the jeep."

Dig That Wombat!

by Phoebe

Wombats are furry animals whose bodies seem designed for digging. They need to dig the tunnels where they sleep all day — and sometimes these tunnels are sixty feet long. To dig such long tunnels, wombats have short, powerful forelegs with strong, flat claws.

At night wombats wake up and come out to eat. Like cows, they eat mostly grass. And, like cows, they have special bacteria in their stomach to help digest it.

It takes a wombat from three to eight hours of chewing each night to get enough to eat!

We ran back to the jeep. "The wombat is a marsupial," Ms. Frizzle explained as we drove along. "What makes marsupials different from other mammals is that they finish growing their young in an exterior pouch, instead of inside the mother."

From the Desk of Ms. Frizzle

Marsupials: Mammals with a Pouch

Marsupials are furry and warm-blooded like other mammals, but they are different in one big important way. Their babies are born before they are ready to live outside their mother.

The tiny, hairless newborns crawl to a special pouch on their mother's belly. Once there, each baby fastens onto a nipple and starts drinking milk.

Even after marsupial babies are big enough to leave the pouch, they still hop back in to sleep, eat, or to escape when danger threatens.

How Many Marsupials?
by Arnold

There are more than 260 different kinds of marsupials, and most of them live in Australia, New Guinea, and Tasmania. The only wild marsupial in the United States is the opossum.

The biggest marsupial is the kangaroo, and the smallest is the marsupial mouse — which would fit in your hand.

Suddenly Tiki yelled, "Stop!" Ms. Frizzle stood on the brakes, and Tiki jumped out of the Magic School Jeep again. She went crashing out into the bush. We heard her rustling around for a minute or two, and then she returned with a nasty-looking creature under her arm. It looked sort of like a cross between a weasel and a dog. Most of its fur was black, but there was white fur under its neck, and it was bald in patches. I made sure I got some good pictures, from a safe distance.

"This is one of our pride and joys," Tiki said with a fond smile at the creature who was thrashing about and flashing its teeth. We all backed up. I sure didn't want to feel those teeth! "The Tasmanian devil. These

guys make such nasty noises, grunts, barks, and screams that they got the name *devil*. They used to be all over Australia, but now they just live here." She was petting the animal as if it were a kitten, though it looked as if it wanted to eat her. She held the Tasmanian devil out to Phoebe, who backed up so fast she stepped on Arnold's toe. It was the meanest-looking creature I had ever seen.

Australia Field Guide
A Useful Devil

Why would anyone call an animal a devil? How about if it looks like a black dog, makes spine-chilling screeches and grunts, and has a terrible bad temper? That's the Tasmanian devil!

Devils are famous for their rowdy feeding behavior — their noise shows who's boss in the pack.

But for all their ferocious appearances, Tasmanian devils are actually helpful scavengers. They clean up the environment by eating dead animals. The devil's powerful jaws and teeth let it eat up every bit of its prey — bones, fur, and all!

"What does he eat?" I asked. I hoped he didn't eat children.

"Ugh, you don't want to know," said Tiki with a big smile. "Anything that's dead. They make terrible noises and fight one another when they find carrion, or dead things. That's how this little cutie got these bald patches."

"He looks kind of dangerous," said Arnold, still holding his toe. "Can he kill?"

"Tasmanian devils do occasionally kill small animals with a big bite on the back of the neck. But they prefer their meat dead. The older and rottener the better!" We all groaned. "They are great at clearing out rodents and dead animals. Nowadays, farmers leave the devils alone, which is good news for the species."

"Do you mean people used to hunt them?" asked Wanda.

"Yeah, they thought the devils were a menace. And not just people, the Tasmanian tiger used to kill them, too." Tiki looked sad.

"Why did the tiger stop killing them?" asked Wanda.

"Unfortunately, the Tasmanian tiger is extinct as far as we know. People used to hunt the tiger to protect their farm animals. But if you kids see a tiger-striped doglike animal, just let me know!"

Australia Field Guide
An Extinct "Tiger"

The Tasmanian tiger wasn't really a cat — it got its name from its dark brown stripes. Except for the stripes, it looked like a large, long dog with a heavy, stiff tail and a big head.

The "tiger" wasn't fierce at all. It kept away from people, and had a shy, nervous temperament — especially compared to its cousin, the Tasmanian devil.

European settlers hunted the tigers to extinction within a century of settlement. The last known Tasmanian tiger died in a zoo on September 7, 1936. Occasionally, people still report seeing the tiger, but sightings have never been officially documented.

Tiki brightened up and set the devil down. The Tasmanian devil started doing a strange spinning dance. Liz, who had been looking curiously at the devil from a nearby rock, leaped back onto the Friz's shoulder.

"Wow!" I said. "What's he doing, spinning around like that?"

"Oh, he's just showing off a bit, trying to scare us. He's not really spinning around, he's just turning from side to side so rapidly that it looks like he's spinning. You know, like in the cartoon." Tiki winked at us. The Tasmanian devil finished spinning and scuttled off into the underbrush. We all climbed back into the jeep.

"Isn't the Tasmanian devil a marsupial, too?" I asked.

"Fair dinkum!" said Tiki. "The Tasmanian devil gives birth to about fifty little rice-sized babies, or joeys, who all crawl as fast as they can to the pouch. The first four babies latch on to the mother's nipples, and they stay there until they're mature enough to live on their own.

At that moment we heard a wild laughing sound that was somehow familiar. It made me shiver. Phoebe jumped, landing on Arnold's other foot.

"The kookaburra!" shouted the Friz. "I knew we'd find him," she said.

"Sounds like that one is heading toward the mainland. And that's where we should go, too," said Tiki.

"Follow that kookaburra! To the bus!" said the Friz.

CHAPTER 3

When we reached a shoreline in Tasmania, the jeep kept going — right into the water. In another instant we were afloat in the Magic School Boat.

Tiki didn't look one bit surprised! She was trailing her hand over the side of the boat as if buses turned into boats every day, a happy smile on her face. I could see why Tiki and the Friz were friends. "Drop anchor!" Tiki suddenly called. And then she dove over the side with all her clothes on.

We crowded to the side to see what she was doing. She stayed underwater a really long time — so long that I started to worry.

Just as Arnold began to say, "Umm, Ms. Frizzle, do you think —" Tiki's head popped out of the water, and next to her head was the strangest-looking creature I'd ever seen. It had a furry head, beautiful dark eyes . . . and a large duckbill.

"Mind throwing us a rope, mate?" sputtered Tiki.

Carlos spotted the rope next to him and threw it over the side. In a flash, Tiki was up, carrying the shaking creature. It was even stranger-looking out of the water. It had

webbed feet, fur, flippers, and a flat tail. It looked like many different animals all in one.

"There is a story that when one of the first settlers was given one of these fellas to look at, he thought it had been sewed together as a joke. He actually looked for stitches." Tiki laughed. "But it's real. It swims, lays eggs, and is as much a mammal as you or I. Ladies and gents, the platypus." Tiki's face was glowing with pride. "We are lucky to see one; normally they are very shy."

"Wow!" I said. "She's beautiful!"

Is It a Bird? Is It a Plane? No, It's a Platypus!

by Wanda

The platypus is possibly the world's weirdest animal.

Despite all its strange features, the platypus is still a mammal! The mother has milk, but does not have nipples like other mammals. Her milk oozes out of glands in her skin, and the babies lap it off her fur.

Platypuses spend all their time in the water, breathing through nostrils in the top of their bills. They feed after dark, and can eat their own weight in food in just one night.

They may sound cute, but watch out! Male platypuses have poisonous spurs on their hind legs, which can kill a dog and cause lots of pain to a human.

"Actually," said Tiki, "this one is a male. See these little horns on the back legs?" She pointed to some bumps on the legs. "These are full of poison." We all looked at one another nervously. I hoped the platypus wasn't going to hurt Tiki, but Tiki gave the creature a hug. "And the platypus is only found in the land down under. One of our two egg-laying mammals."

"What's the other one?" asked Wanda.

"According to my research, that would be the echidna," I said proudly.

"That's right, D.A." said Tiki. "Maybe if we're lucky we'll find one on the mainland. But meanwhile I want to put our friend back in the water so he can get on with his business." She slowly lowered the platypus into the water and we watched him swim off. "Carry on, mates!" she called, and we continued to chug along.

"Wow, that really was interesting," said Arnold. He took a picture of the swimming platypus.

"It's another Down Under Wonder!" said Carlos.

Before the platypus had disappeared

from our view, the boat was hitting ground and Tiki was leaping over the side again.

"Look here, look here!" she called out as she stood up in the shallow water. She was holding something in her hand.

She climbed on deck, opened her hand, and showed us a small frog.

"We have frogs, too," said Ralphie.

"But this here's not just any frog," said Tiki. "This is a gastric breeding frog. She actually hatches her tadpoles in her stomach. She stops eating and stops producing stomach juices for about eight weeks until the tadpoles hatch. Then they hop out of her mouth!" Tiki held the frog out to Carlos, who was snapping pictures. Then she lowered the frog back into the water.

"Just another of the wonders of Oz," said the Friz. "And thar she lies!" she announced with a grand gesture.

We looked over the side of the boat and saw the rocky coast of mainland Australia. What a wonderful trip!

CHAPTER 4

Before Tiki was dry, the boat had turned back into the Magic School Jeep. "We are on the mainland now, mates," said Tiki. "We're not going to have time to stop much because we're headed for a special place to meet some animals. But I want you all to take a Captain Cook as we drive across the south of the continent, and take pictures of any interesting animals you see."

Aussie Dictionary

CAPTAIN COOK: A look (take a Captain Cook around). This is a rare, silly phrase.

Ms. Frizzle turned down a small road that led through a forest. It smelled heavenly. "These are eucalyptus trees," Tiki told us. She took a deep sniff. "Ahh."

The Cough Drop Tree
by Tim

The leaves of the eucalyptus tree contain an oil that will clear your sinuses and help drain your nose. That's why eucalyptus oil is used in many medicines — including cough drops.

Native to Australia, eucalyptus trees grow well in any dry climate and have been planted all over the world.

"Eucalyptus trees are also known as 'gum trees' in a certain familiar song," said the Friz with a smile.

Aussie Dictionary

GUM TREE: Eucalyptus tree

"Great, we must be close to the kookaburra!" said Arnold. He looked up and let out a startled yelp. "What's that?" he asked Tiki.

"Quick, take out your cameras," said Tiki. We looked up at where Arnold was pointing. I couldn't believe my eyes. It looked something like a little squirrel, but it was flying. Could this be a kookaburra? I snapped a couple of pictures.

"Who was that masked animal?" asked Phoebe.

"That was a sugar glider," said Tiki. I felt a little disappointed that we hadn't found the mysterious kookaburra yet, but the sugar glider was really cool.

"How does he fly like that?" Keesha asked.

"Actually, he's gliding. There are flaps of skin between his arms and his body, kind of like a cape, that catch the air and allow him to glide like a kite. He can glide up to one hundred yards, which is almost as good as flying!"

"Why is he called a sugar glider?" asked Phoebe. "Is he sweet?"

"He's not sweet — he'll give you a nasty bite if you try and grab him — but he likes to eat sweet things, like honey and tree gum, so the Aborigines named him *sugar glider*. The sugar glider is also a marsupial."

Aussie Dictionary

ABORIGINE: A native Australian; the people who lived in Australia before European set–tlers arrived.

Australia Field Guide
The Sugar Glider — It's So Sweet

It's called the sugar glider, but it's really a possum that can launch itself from one tree to another. A loose flap of skin between its hand and its toe spreads out and lets the animal glide smoothly — sometimes for a distance of up to 160 feet! Sugar gliders almost never touch the ground.

I noticed that the trees we were passing now were really huge. "Wow," I said. "Look at the size of these trees!"

"These are called karri trees. People used to cut them down for their wood. It's an especially hard and durable wood. But now they're protected," Tiki said.

"I think these are the biggest trees I've ever seen," said Carlos.

"They can grow as tall as our California redwoods," the Friz added.

"We have to be extra careful with our forests here in Australia. They make up only five percent of the whole continent, and a lot of animals depend on them for homes."

I was hoping the kookaburra was one of those animals. I was keeping a sharp lookout — and keeping an ear out for that crazy laughing sound, too.

We were speeding along at a good clip when Keesha yelled, "Oh, look! It's a baby koala riding piggyback!" Ms. Frizzle slowed down, so we could get a good look.

Tiki laughed. "Ahh yes, the famous koala. Like almost all of our mammals, they're marsupials. The koala is a cousin of the wombat. She's awfully cuddly looking, with all that beautiful fur."

"Can we stop and pet one?" Arnold asked shyly.

"I'm afraid not. Koalas are pretty solitary creatures. They spend most of their time up in the trees and they live completely on a diet of leaves. And although they look sweet, they really aren't very friendly to humans."

As Tiki was talking, Ms. Frizzle parked the Magic School Jeep. We clambered out, cameras in hand.

"This looks like a great spot. Time to hit

the ground and find some more animals!" Tiki said.

"Will we see a kookaburra?" Ralphie asked excitedly.

"Well, you never know where that kookaburra will turn up!" said Tiki. Just then we heard that laugh again.

"It's a kookaburra!" yelled Keesha.

"That sounds like one all right," said Tiki. "Let's go find him!"

"I think we're in the right place," whispered Wanda.

From the Desk of Ms. Frizzle

Koala Bare Facts

The koala is not a bear at all, but another marsupial mammal. The name *koala* comes from an Aboriginal phrase that means "no drink." The koala gets the moisture it needs from the eucalyptus leaves that it eats. It is one of the only animals that can digest the bitter toxins in eucalyptus leaves. It has extra-long intestines to give it time to digest the leaves.

CHAPTER 5

We started trekking through the bush, trying to keep up with Tiki. She didn't seem to notice all the roots, rocks, and prickers. We reached a clearing and Tiki turned to face us. We were glad she stopped because we were all out of breath.

"The biggest problem facing our wild-life — next to human beings — is ferals. You ankle biters know what a feral is?" She looked around at our faces. Nobody said anything.

Aussie Dictionary

ANKLE BITER: Young child

"Ferals are animals that were brought here by European settlers. They're creatures that aren't native, and in my opinion they just don't belong in Australia. They're animals that are common where you live, like rabbits, foxes, goats, pigs, cats, and dogs. Once people brought them here and they escaped into the wild, they caused terrible problems for our native species. They eat the food that the native wildlife eats, and some of them hunt and eat our native wildlife. So several Australian zoos have worked to breed our native animals and put them back into the wilderness where they can keep feral animals out. This is one of those areas." I looked around. It didn't look any different from other places we'd driven by.

"Get your cameras out," said Tiki. "We're going to see some interesting creatures."

She moved to a hollow log and picked up one end, gently shaking it until a sleepy, long-nosed, furry animal with a bushy tail slid out. I wondered how she had known which log to shake. "This is a numbat. He eats some ants, but mostly termites. You're very lucky to see him because there aren't that many numbats left." Our cameras clicked. Tiki gently slid the sleepy numbat back into its log.

"Go ahead and have a look around," she said. "It's perfectly safe here." I thought Tiki had some strange ideas of what was safe, but it was great to run around and look for things.

I was really hoping to be the one to spot the kookaburra, whatever it might be. We all peered into hollow logs and peeked behind rocks until suddenly I heard Wanda scream. Everybody rushed over to where she was standing, next to a rock.

Tiki was scooping something up from behind the rock. "I'll bet you never saw the likes of this before!" She set the animal down in front of us. It looked like a porcupine. It took one look at us and curled up into a big spiky ball. I couldn't believe Tiki had held such a prickly creature without hurting herself. She definitely seemed to have a special way with animals.

"An echidna!" Phoebe said proudly, looking in my Australia field guide.

"Ridgy-didge!" said Tiki.

Aussie Dictionary

RIDGY–DIDGE: The honest truth

Tiki looked at the curled-up ball of spikes. "Aww," said Tiki, "I'm not going to hurt you." She sounded amused. "He just does that to protect himself. We've got lots of echidnas in Australia because they can survive all over the place. Watch this." She took a stick and gently prodded the echidna. It burrowed into the ground until nothing was sticking out but some very sharp-looking needles.

"Nobody would want to eat a pincushion like that for dinner! The echidna eats ants and termites with its very long, sticky tongue. And, just like the platypus, the echidna is a mammal that lays eggs. The mother keeps the eggs in a small, temporary pouch. The young hatch and stay in the pouch until they are about three weeks old."

Australia Field Guide
The Spiny Anteater

The echidna (pronounced uh-KID-nuh), also called the spiny anteater, looks like a porcupine. It's covered with short hairs to keep it warm, and long, sharp spines to protect it from enemies.

An echidna lives entirely on ants and termites. The tip of its nose has cells that can detect electrical signals from an insect's nervous system. That's how it finds ant and termite nests.

Then the hungry anteater tears into the nest with strong claws and catches the scurrying insects with its sticky tongue.

"Well, kids, it's time to get back in the jeep if we're going to make it to our campsite before dark." Tiki took off toward the jeep.

"Wait!" Ralphie called. Tiki turned mid-stride and looked back at all of us.

"Where's the kookaburra?" Ralphie asked. "We really want to find one!"

"Oh. The kookaburra must have taken off somewhere. No worries! He'll be back. Come on, move along now." She hurried off. We looked at the Friz.

"Well, a kookaburra must do what a kookaburra must do," said the Friz, "and a class must do what a class must do — we must set up camp! Off to the Back of Beyond, the Never Never Country — that sunbathed land of red sandy dunes, black gidgee trees, turquoise blue horizons, and star-filled nights." The Friz was warming to her subject. We walked after the Friz and Tiki through the trees.

Aussie Dictionary

NO WORRIES: No problem; it'll be okay
NEVER NEVER: The bush, the outback

"Camp!" said Arnold. "Oh, no, I'm not sleeping in all this prickly stuff!"

"It won't be prickly where we're going, Arnold. We're headed for the outback," said Tiki. "Its pretty barren out there and there aren't too many bugs."

Arnold looked relieved.

"There may be some snakes, though. . . ." said Tiki with a mischievous smile. Arnold looked worried again.

"Come on, class, off to the Magic School Helicopter — we want to get there before dark!"

CHAPTER 6

The helicopter landed just as the sun was setting. We piled out. "Quick," said the Friz from inside. "Let's set up camp." We turned around and the Magic School Helicopter was a bungalow. When the Friz says "quick," she means it. I looked up. The sky was a beautiful turquoise on one side and a magnificent orange on the other.

"Chow time!" called the Friz. She was unloading sacks of dough, tomatoes, cheese, graham crackers, Australian chocolate bars, and marshmallows. Outback pizza and Aussie treats! The Friz is the greatest.

We rolled the pizza dough on the sloped

side of the bus-bungalow, chopped the toma-toes, sprinkled on cheese, and set the pizzas over the fire that Tiki, Carlos, Wanda, and Arnold had built.

Arnold may not have wanted a field trip, but he was definitely having fun now.

"That hits the spot, mates!" said Tiki when she tasted the pizza.

It was the best pizza I ever had! After the pizza, Tiki put the billy on the fire and we had Aussie tea and s'mores. When Tiki saw the

Aussie chocolate, she said it was really "dinkie die!" We started feeling like real Australians.

Aussie Dictionary

BILLY: A can in which water is boiled over a campfire to make tea
DINKIE DIE: The real thing, an original

As the campfire died down, Ms. Frizzle took out sets of kangaroo pajamas for all of us,

and we crawled into our sleeping bags. (Tiki called them "swags.") It was so warm and dry, we didn't even need the bungalow. Tiki showed us something called a didgeridoo, a native Australian instrument that looked like a big painted log, and she said it made eerie music. But she could not play it for us, because it is sacred to the Aborigines. We looked up at the stars — there were billions of them. I'd never seen so many in my whole life.

"Wow," said Arnold. "This is great."

As I drifted off to sleep, I thought I heard the kookaburra's laugh — but it must have been Wanda and Keesha, giggling.

The next morning we woke up under the biggest sky I've ever seen. After a minute, I noticed that we weren't alone. We were surrounded by a mob of very big kangaroos. I jumped to my feet. The rest of the kids were still sleeping, but Tiki and the Friz were up and they smiled at me.

"Everyone up!" Ms. Friz said quietly. "We've got company — and you'll be hopping mad if you miss them!"

Australia Field Guide

Q: What Has Big Feet and Jumps?
A: A Kangaroo

Scientists call the kangaroo family *Macro-pods,* which means "big foot." Look at a kangaroo and you'll see why. If a kangaroo went shoe shopping, it would need a size 30!

There are at least 69 different types, or species, of kangaroo. Besides kangaroos, some other members of the family are wallabies, wallaroos, pademelons, and tree kangaroos.

Gradually all the kids sat up in their sleeping bags, rubbing their eyes. Carlos and Wanda saw the kangaroos first. They grinned.

"Wow!" said Carlos.

Phoebe, Keesha, and Ralphie looked too sleepy to do more than stare. Arnold ducked back inside his sleeping bag.

Tiki began passing around buttered rolls and cartons of milk that we ate and drank right in our sleeping bags. "Tiki's Luxury Outback Tours, breakfast in bed included," Tiki said with a laugh. The Friz was unloading something from the bungalow. I wondered what she was up to.

As we ate our breakfast, we studied the kangaroos around us. There were about thirty of them, and they ranged from reddish-brown to grayish in color. Several of them were very small and were sticking close to their mothers. But most of them were bigger than us. Many of them were medium tall, and there was one really large one. He was about the size of a grown-up, professional football player. I could understand why Arnold had ducked back into his sleeping bag. I felt a little nervous myself.

"These are red kangaroos," Tiki explained. "They are the largest kangaroos of all the kangaroo family. That big boomer over there is the dominant male." Tiki pointed at the football player. "And those three medium-grayish females must be the breeding does." She pointed to the next-largest kangaroos. "And the rest are all joeys — children of all different sizes and ages." Now that I looked carefully, I could see that two mothers had baby kangaroos in their pouches, too.

Australia Field Guide
The Biggest "Big Foot"

The red kangaroo is the largest living marsupial, weighing in at about 200 pounds and measuring up to six and a half feet tall.

Red kangaroos are the "camels" of Australia. As long as they have green grass to eat, they don't have to drink water at all!

Just to make things a little confusing, red kangaroos are not all red: some, especially females, are a blue–gray color.

Meanwhile, the Friz was unwrapping the big bundle she'd brought out of the bungalow, as we all watched curiously. It was a bunch of metal rods with springs on the bottom — pogo sticks!

Aussie Dictionary

BOOMER: Male kangaroo
DOE: Female kangaroo
MOB: Group of kangaroos

"Time to join the mob, campers!" the Friz sang out. She climbed on one of the pogo sticks and started hopping. Soon she was really flying. Two of the kangaroos hopped alongside her. They were easily keeping up with her. She hopped back. "To the pogo sticks, class!"

We all grabbed pogo sticks and started hopping. It took a little practice, but we got the hang of it. The kangaroos watched curiously. Ralphie was the best because he had a pogo stick at home. He gave the rest of us advice.

"And now, we're off to spend the morning with the kangaroos! Let's go!"

"Umm, I think I'll wait here. . . ." said Arnold. He was looking a little green.

Two kangaroos hopped over next to him and looked at him.

"All right, all right, I'm going." Arnold took off as fast as he could, looking worriedly over his shoulder. We all laughed and hopped off after him.

CHAPTER 7

Hopping with the kangaroos was good exercise. The sun wasn't even up yet and I was getting tired and thirsty. But the kangaroos kept going, and they looked very rested.

"Don't they ever stop?" panted Phoebe, hopping next to Tiki.

"Kangaroos can hop for a long time. Hopping takes less effort than running, and the kangaroos use their energy more slowly than we do," Ms. Frizzle said between hops.

"Oh, great," said Arnold. "How do we ask them to stop?"

"They'll stop soon — they'll be wanting their breakfast," Tiki said. And sure enough, we could see that the large boomer was coming to a stop near some thick grass. We hopped off our pogo sticks and flopped down to rest next to a swampy-looking water hole.

Hip-Hoppin' Roos

by D.A.

Of all the animals in the world, only a few get around by hopping. Of these, kangaroos may be the champion hoppers. They use their strong legs and long feet to speed along, hopping at up to 40 miles per hour.

To move slowly, kangaroos have to use a whole other form of locomotion. First, they balance on their small front paws and tail. Then they swing their hind legs forward like the pendulum of a clock.

We took out our own water bottles and drank as we watched the kangaroos. Both of the little joeys were out of their mothers' pouches and all the kangaroos were grazing on the bristly-looking grass.

"Is that tough grass the only thing they eat?" Ralphie asked.

"Yes. Kangaroos have special stomachs that can break down these tough grasses," Tiki answered.

"How come the third doe doesn't have a joey in her pouch?" asked Keesha.

"She probably has a newborn," Tiki replied. "When the joeys are first born, they're only the size of a bumblebee. They've got to grow in the pouch until they're big enough to get out." It was hard to imagine creatures as big as these kangaroos starting out so small.

One of the big young boomers was approaching the biggest male. Suddenly they were face-to-face with their forearms locked, like wrestlers.

"What's he doing?" shrieked Phoebe.

"Oh, that's how male kangaroos fight to

see who's boss. But I wouldn't worry too much. This young boomer is nowhere near ready. He's just practicing. When they really get going they use their powerful hind legs to kick while balancing on their tails," Tiki said. The young boomer was already scampering off.

Suddenly Tiki jumped up and ran over to the largest male. She locked her arms with his and started wrestling. We couldn't believe our eyes. They were swaying back and forth until finally Tiki twisted free, giving the kangaroo a friendly pat on the arm. She walked back to us, laughing when she saw our shocked faces. "Well, it's a great way to stay in shape when you're far away from a gym." She calmly sat down and took a drink of water. I had never met anyone like Tiki before!

All in all, it was a peaceful morning. We lolled in the grass and watched the young joeys playing. The sun was coming up and the sky was turning a deep, rich blue. It was getting very hot!

I was just dozing off a little, thinking about the sound of the kookaburra's laugh

and trying to imagine what kind of creature would make that sound. Something big. Something so huge it made the ground shake. My eyes popped open. The ground *was* shaking!

The big boomer was thumping the ground with his back legs. The whole area vibrated with the power of his thumps. It sounded like down under thunder!

"What's going on?" Carlos asked, when suddenly the kangaroos took off. The mamas waited for the little joeys to jump into their pouches, then bounded off after the others.

"Dingoes!" Tiki yelled. "Grab your pogo sticks and head for the hills!"

I couldn't see any hills, but I grabbed my stick and started hopping after the mob. The kangaroos were going so fast that I couldn't possibly keep up with them. And I wasn't the only one. Suddenly I heard a horn, and the Magic School Jeep, piloted by Liz, was pulling up next to us. We gratefully climbed in. My legs felt like they'd never hop again.

"Follow those kangaroos!" the Friz said,

and we took off after the kangaroos in the distance.

"Look!" shouted Ralphie, pointing to the hopping mob of kangaroos. Two pogo sticks flashed in the sun. Keesha and Arnold had kept up with the mob!

"Can we catch them?" Phoebe asked Ms. Frizzle.

"Not at the speed they're going!" said the Friz. She didn't look at all worried.

Carlos did, though. "Look back this way!" he cried. He was pointing out from the back of the jeep. We all turned around. What looked like two big dogs were running after the kangaroos — and us.

"Those are dingoes?" asked Ralphie. "They look like ordinary dogs."

"Dingoes are wild dogs. We think they came to Australia about fifteen thousand years ago with some Asian sailors. Dingoes don't get fed like your dogs, so they have to hunt. But no worries — it looks like these poor dingoes are going to stay hungry today,"

Tiki said. The dogs were slowing down. Finally, they turned around and trotted away.

Australia Field Guide
A Dog Called Dingo

Dingoes are wild dogs that live only in Australia. They usually hunt alone or in pairs and live mostly on small mammals, reptiles, and insects.

When small game is scarce, however, dingoes band together in packs and tackle large animals like sheep and even kangaroos.

Now that the dingoes were gone, we watched the kangaroos again. They had slowed down quite a bit, but they were still hopping. I thought about how quickly the mob had taken off and how the joeys had disappeared into their mothers' pockets.

"How did the joeys know which one was their mother?" I asked.

"The mothers would have let any joey hop into her pouch during danger," said Tiki. "Makes things easier."

We caught up to our mob of kangaroos on a patch of rocks. There, lying down with the other kangaroos, were Arnold and Keesha, very out of breath. "Are you all right?" I asked them as we all piled out of the jeep. Keesha nodded happily and Arnold gave a big grin.

"That" — he panted a few times — "was fun!"

"Good hopping, kids!" Tiki said with admiration.

Many of the kangaroos were resting in the little patches of shade. They were all panting like Keesha and Arnold, and many of them were licking their forearms.

"Why are they doing that?" asked Wanda.

"That's how they cool themselves down. The panting helps them give off some heat, just as it does for other mammals. And the thin skin in their forearms makes it easier for the coolness of their wet tongues to spread throughout their bodies," Tiki said.

"Well, I'm sure glad they're safe," Keesha said.

Some of the kangaroos were lying down and going to sleep.

Ms. Frizzle smiled at Arnold. "You've learned to hop, Arnold."

Arnold looked thoughtful. "Yeah, I guess so. I was so worried about the kangaroos that I forgot I didn't know how to use the pogo stick that well."

"Sometimes we learn a lot about another species when we hop in their shoes for a while!" the Friz said with a wink. We all groaned. No more hopping for us.

CHAPTER 8

The Magic School Bus was taking off again in its jet form. Our early morning run with the mob had left us hot and tired. I was ready to sit down for a while. "As we fly over the land of Oz, I want to point out some things to you," Tiki said.

"If you look out your windows, you'll see a tropical rain forest below. This is one of our most precious resources."

"I thought Australia was all eucalyptus trees and bush," said Carlos.

"As a matter of fact, Australia has twelve different ecological regions, though the

73

rain forest is primarily eucalyptus. It might be one of the smaller rain forests of the world, but it is very important. Some cousins of our kangaroo friends, the tree kangaroos, can only be found in this rain forest. We only have twenty-five percent of our rain forest left, but now we are protecting it."

As the jet banked sharply, the rain forest disappeared from view.

"We're flying over the tropical savannah now," Tiki said. "Ms. Frizzle, can you set us

down on the coast? I have to get off to meet my next group," she continued, "but I wanted to show you one last impressive creature."

Would it be the kookaburra? I hoped so.

We had landed next to a sand bank. As we got out of the jet, I looked up. On top of the sand bank was the largest animal I'd ever seen. It was longer than four of us kids together and was covered with scales. If this thing was the kookaburra, I wasn't so sure I wanted to meet it!

"Be quiet, you don't want to wake up this fella," Tiki said, leaning casually on the creature's back. At that moment it lifted its great head and we could see that it was a crocodile. He blinked his eyes sleepily. Tiki grinned and the crocodile opened a mouth full of sharp teeth. His mouth was big enough to swallow her whole, but she didn't move.

"I think this would be a good time to get back in the jet," said the Friz, a slightly anxious note in her voice. We didn't need to be asked twice.

"Could I catch a ride to the beach?" Tiki asked.

Beach! We all looked at Ms. Frizzle hopefully.

"That sounds like a wonderful way to end our Australian adventure. After all, Australian beaches are supposed to be some of the best in the whole world! Luckily, I packed my cozzie." Ms. Frizzle held up her kangaroo-print bathing suit. "You should all have your own bathing suits in your packs." The Friz thinks of everything.

Salty, the Man-eating Croc
by Carlos

It's the largest reptile in the world, growing up to 20 feet long. It lives in coastal areas and rivers and eats fish, turtles, birds, and other animals that come by.

For all its bad reputation as a man-eater, the Australian saltwater crocodile has only eaten about twelve people in all of Australian history. These were folks who were foolish enough to get too close – so if you're in Australia, give this croc a wide berth!

We drove along the beach, until Tiki asked Ms. Frizzle to stop at a small inlet. We all got out and walked to the shore. Tiki began making some strange noises, and suddenly a big fat animal that looked a lot like a seal poked its head out of the water.

"How did you do that?" asked Arnold.

"Oh, just a little tour guide secret," said Tiki, with a wink at the Friz. "This is a dugong, or sea cow. Like whales and dolphins, she's a mammal who spends her whole life in the sea. On our northern coasts we have the largest population of dugong in the world."

We looked at the dugong, which was now flopping on the sand. She was enormous and had a funny flat face.

Are There Mermaids in Australia?
by Keesha

Not really, but a long time ago, people thought there were. Dugongs, also called sea cows, were the mistaken mermaids.

How can a big animal called a sea cow look like a mermaid? First, it swims very gracefully and looks beautiful underwater. Second, a mother dugong holds her baby in a way that looks like a human mother cradling her child. And last, sea cows mourn for their mates, which reminds people of human wives.

Dugongs are shy plant-eaters and have their own language, which sounds like chirps and barks.

"What are those holes on the top of her head?" asked Tim.

"Those are her nostrils. They sit on a fleshy lip that can curl up to make breathing easier on the water's surface." Tiki patted the enormous creature on her head. "Go on back now, luv. Thanks for visiting." The dugong splashed back into the sea.

Suddenly Tiki reached down and grabbed something in the sand. "Look out!" she cried.

She was grinning and waving a snake around, looking like a kid with a flag. "Oh, super! This is a poisonous sea snake. I haven't seen one of these in a long time." We all stood perfectly still, afraid of what the snake might do. "Our sea snakes are mighty poisonous."

We all looked worriedly at the Friz. Ms. Frizzle was smiling from ear to ear. "OK, Tiki, I think we all got a good look!"

Tiki was gazing at the snake happily, but she looked up then. "Oh," she said, noticing our scared faces. "Right." She let the snake go, and it slithered back into the water. As soon as the snake had disappeared, we all ran back into the bus as fast as we could. I was beginning to wonder whether Tiki and the Friz were related.

We drove along the coast some more until we came to a beautiful beach. "This is where I get out!" said Tiki.

I felt really sad. Tiki had taught us so much. Even though she hadn't led us to the kookaburra, I wanted to give her something to say thank-you. Suddenly I remembered my old science fair medal, still in my pocket.

"Here, Tiki, you're the best tour guide around. Will you take this?"

"D.A.!" said Tiki. "That's the nicest present anyone ever gave me." She pinned it to her safari shirt.

"Bye, Tiki," we called. "Thanks for everything."

"Come back soon, mates," she called over her shoulder as she walked away. We saw a big tour bus full of kids waiting for her.

"Wait!" yelled Arnold. "What about the kookaburra?"

"Oh, no worries! You'll know it when you see it! And I think you'll see it soon!" said Tiki as she jumped into the new bus.

"But when?" yelled Ralphie.

Tiki just waved back at him as her bus pulled off onto the road.

Maybe the kookaburra was imaginary after all. Maybe that missing "K" page in the field guide had some other animal's listing.

We waded out into the water, our fears of poisonous snakes and man-eating crocodiles forgotten. It had been a long, hot day and the water felt wonderful. Soon we even forgot about the kookaburra.

CHAPTER 9

All too soon, the Friz called, "Back to the bus!" We climbed on, but Arnold was missing.

"There he is!" shouted Carlos. We all looked out the window to see Arnold digging in the sand for crabs. "Hey, Arnold," Carlos called. "Are you under the spell of down under? The bus is leaving without you!"

Arnold flashed a big smile and ran to climb on the bus. The sun was setting and Ms. Frizzle was just starting up the bus when suddenly we heard a strange laughing sound. Then a second laughing voice joined in and finally there was a whole chorus. The laughter seemed to be coming from all around us. We pressed our noses to the windows, not knowing what we'd see. I sure hoped it was friendly. It had us surrounded.

"Look up!" said Ms. Frizzle. "We didn't find just one kookaburra, we found the whole gang."

As the bus pulled out, a whole group of beautiful birds flew next to us. We could see their creamy white bellies and their funny oversized heads. I never would have guessed that such eerie sounds could come from such a beautiful bird! As I hunted in my bag for my camera, I found the missing page of the field guide.

Australia Field Guide
Laughing Kookaburra

The Kookaburra is a famous bird known for its cackling laugh. It "laughs" like that to mark its territory. Kookaburras have short thick bodies, large heads, and a dark streak over their eyes. They live in Tasmania and eastern Australia and feed on insects, mice, and lizards.

"We have an honor guard escort," Ms. Frizzle announced. "Class, let's sing our song."

As we broke into the kookaburra song, the Magic School Jet took off for home.

Back in the classroom, we had a wonderful time setting up our science fair booth on Australian wildlife. We brought in sand and eucalyptus branches. The smell reminded us of our great trip.

We hung a big map of Australia on the wall and traced our route across the continent. Near each stop we pinned up our wildlife snapshots of the animals we'd seen. Underneath them we hung entries from the Australia field guide. We built a fake campfire with a billy for tea sitting on it, and Keesha set up a tape of the kookaburra laughing that played while the judges were in the room. We gave each judge an Australian chocolate bar and copies of our class riddle book that we wrote together on our trip back home. Each of us wore our kangaroo pajamas and spoke our best Aussie slang!

Carlos had made a giant kookaburra out of papier-mâche. We hung it in the middle of the room. Arnold said that way we'd never have to go all the way around the world to find one again.

We worked hard — I had a science fair

medal to replace, since I had given my first one to Tiki. And guess what! Ms. Frizzle says it was the chocolate bars that did it, but we won! I got a new science fair medal — but the real prize was a trip down under that I'll never forget.

Class Riddle Book

What do you call a kangaroo wanna-be?
A wallaby! (A wallaby is a small kangaroo.)
(by Wanda)

What do you get when you put a pair of eyeglasses in a cup of milk?
A sea cow. (by D.A.)

What has a bill like a duck, a tail like a beaver, lays egg like a frog, swims like a fish, and is covered with fur?
A platypus. (by Phoebe)

What do you say if someone tells you she has a frog in her throat?
You must be a gastric breeding frog!
(by Carlos)

Which family names all its children Joey?

The marsupial family. (by Keesha)

Who only needs to add pepper when he eats his dinner?

The saltwater crocodile. (by Arnold)